IMAGINE!
THOUGHT-PROVOKING POETRY

VOICES OF THE FUTURE

Edited By Allie Jones

First published in Great Britain in 2021 by:

Young Writers
Remus House
Coltsfoot Drive
Peterborough
PE2 9BF
Telephone: 01733 890066
Website: www.youngwriters.co.uk

Printed and bound in the UK by BookPrintingUK
Website: www.bookprintinguk.com
YB0467C

FOREWORD

Since 1991, here at Young Writers we have celebrated the awesome power of creative writing, especially in young adults, where it can serve as a vital method of expressing their emotions and views about the world around them. In every poem we see the effort and thought that each pupil published in this book has put into their work and by creating this anthology we hope to encourage them further with the ultimate goal of sparking a life-long love of writing.

Our latest competition for secondary school students, Imagine, challenged young writers to delve into their imaginations to conjure up alternative worlds where anything is possible. We provided a range of speculative questions to inspire them from 'what if kids ruled the world?' to 'what if everyone was equal?' or they were free to use their own ideas. The result is this creative collection of poetry that imagines endless possibilities and explores the consequences both good and bad.

We encourage young writers to express themselves and address subjects that matter to them, which sometimes means writing about sensitive or contentious topics. If you have been affected by any issues raised in this book, details on where to find help can be found at www.youngwriters.co.uk/info/other/contact-lines

CONTENTS

Cottingham High School, Cottingham

George Pay (14)	73
Jacob Gray (14)	74
Evie Bott (14)	76
Ethan Ramsey	77
Maisy O'Neil (14)	78

Denton Community College, Denton

Micky Reynolds (11)	79
Marko Gotovac (11)	80
Ruby Hill (11)	81
Kaitlyn McCormack (11)	82
Ava Lynch (12)	83
Cody Tunnicliffe (11)	84
Skye Kay (12)	85
Luke Jones (11)	86

Dyson Perrins CE Academy, Malvern

Victoria Cross (12)	87
Cindy-Louise McNally (12)	88
Megan Kimber (12)	90
Danielle Cochrane (13)	91

Eden Boys' School, Preston

Abdullah Patel (11)	92
Abdur-Rahman Wadie (11)	94
Aamir Motala (12)	96
Ibraheem Bhula	97
Mohammed Rayan Zafar (12)	98
Aahil Chughtai (11)	99
Fazale Subhan (11)	100

Exhall Grange School, Ash Green

Ekjyot Bhambra (14)	101
Joshua Powis (12)	102
Amelia Smith (13)	104
Lucy Rees (13)	106

Kyla Lawrence (13)	108
George Williams (14)	110
Nathan Field (14)	112
Grace Wheeler (12)	113
Lucy Hibbert (14)	114
Cian Orme (11)	115
Daniel Bugg (14)	116
Lainey Milligan (13)	117
Sophie McNally (15)	118
Lexie Todd (11)	119
Kirath Mann (11)	120
Tyla Basra (13)	121
Maximus Warwood (12)	122
Harry Rawden (11)	123

Fitzharrys School, Abingdon

Marika Wasikiewicz (11)	124
Daniella Jones (12)	126

Great Academy Ashton, Ashton-Under-Lyne

Laura Ferreira de Oliveira (13)	127
Elisha Richards (13)	128
Imaan Ahsan (13)	130
Skyler Shaw (13)	132
Vidhi Shah (13)	133
Olivia Hayhurst (12)	134
Zulaykha Sheikh (12)	135
Afsana Siddiqa (13)	136

Guilsborough Academy, Guilsborough

Maisy Montgomery (11)	137
Amelia-Rose Montgomery (12)	138
Maisie Given (14)	140
Brooke Dibra (12)	141
Hannah Tilt (15)	142
Katie Nicholls (13)	143
Oliver Green (14)	144
Yuvraj Singh (12)	145
Ashley Prickett (11)	146

Hagley Catholic High School, Hagley

Daniel Chukwuemeka Duru (13)	147
Poppy Mullaney (13)	148
Elle Ashe (13)	152
Theresa Collins (13)	154
Sofia Iantosca (13)	156

John Leggott College, Scunthorpe

Jaymie-Leigh Brennan (16)	157
Stephanie Papworth (17)	158

Kingdown Community School, Warminster

Penny Russell (16)	161
Tia Daniels (15)	162
Vivienne Simcox (12)	164
Danny Loseli (11)	165
Amber-Rose Cullen (11)	166

Landau Forte Academy Amington, Tamworth

Luke Cockle	167
Lucy Angel Molloy (14)	168
Olivia Statham (13)	169
Libby Ashley	170
Seth Cordell	171
Ruby Lewis (13)	172

Lincoln Castle Academy, Lincoln

Sophie Howard (11)	173
Lilly Killingsworth (12)	174
Kaden Portasman (12)	175
Lacey Farnsworth (11)	176
Carley Barley (11)	177
Scarlett Richardson (12)	178
Bradley Portasman (12)	179
Sereina Smith (11)	180

THE POEMS

Imagine

Imagine a world without COVID-19
A world without masks where smiles can be seen
Imagine a world where touching wasn't a crime
People hanging out in big groups all of the time

Imagine laughing children blowing bubbles and having fun
Instead of being forced into grade-level ones
Imagine a world without COVID-19
Where we could travel abroad and not have to quarantine

The virus is a monster spreading all kinds of dangers
But the worse part is it's made us all strangers
But we must imagine and we must keep on believing
There will be an end to this time that we are grieving

There will again be a time with football fans in a big crowd
Cheering, embracing and shouting too loud
There will again be a wedding with a bride and a groom
Surrounded live by their guests and not on Zoom

There will again be a time kids can sit on grandparents' laps
And we won't ever worry about 2-metre gaps.
We will throw out the wipes and the last latex glove
And be allowed to give hugs to all those we love.

Ruby Read
ACS International School, Cobham

Twenty-Four

Twenty-four
The waves crash against the pillow-white soft sand
Twenty-three
Blissfully, I lie down and stare at the blazing sun
Twenty-two
My eyes flit from cloud to cloud, picturing fire-breathing
dragons and flying pigs
Twenty-one
I take a gulp of air, fresh, hazy, divine
Twenty
My hands grab the air, trying to grasp onto something to
anchor me
Nineteen
The sharp, icy water shocks my feet, as it seeps in through
the tide
Eighteen
Rolling over into the sea, my body goes numb from the cold
Seventeen
My face is submerged by the salty water, as I lie face-first in
the ocean of possibilities
Sixteen
Pushing and pulling, I make my way through the clear oasis
that is the water
Fifteen
My eyes flutter open to see the crystal-blue sea of wonders

Fourteen

I gaze, starstruck, amazed by the workings of Mother Nature

Thirteen

My hands scramble along the sand, trying to hold onto the slug-like substance

Twelve

The crest of the water pushes me up to the surface, and I gasp for air, not realising my own instability in this fragile life

Eleven

Floating isolated in the Moana, I have never felt so untroubled

Ten

Not a single thought passes through my head; not a worry or bother

Nine

As if on cue, I feel a sharp pain in my foot: a fish nibbling at my toes

Eight

The fish is bright, colourful, at peace, everything I aspired to be in my short yet fulfilled life

Seven

I dive back under the deep to try to discover more of this vibrant life before I lose it

Six

The kelp envelops me, the wildlife seems wonderstruck by my human body, and I feel the passion for the beings of the sea

Five
The ocean is a child of nature, created by Earth to amaze
and infatuate mankind
Four

Pushing off the slick, slimy sand, I impel out of the water
shaped like an arch; feeling like a
mermaid
Three
All rational thinking escapes from my head, as I realise this
is the last time I would take a
breath
Two
One final time, I open my mouth, and the oxygen travels
through my lungs and out again
One...

Lucy Crowther
ACS International School, Cobham

What Is It Like To Be Immortal?

What is it like? you may think,
Well let me tell you it isn't just a blink,
I've seen and felt things that many can't!
Although it's not something many can grant,

What is it like? you may think,
To feel the strong warm touch of a bullet,
What is it like you may think
To feel the water grab you as the rocks yell your name,

What is it like? you may think,
To watch the ones you love fall away,
As you go back into the sadness that will sway -
You start to feel regret and sadness,
Until it eats you whole and turns it into madness!

Although I live forever,
I sometimes stop and think -
What is it like to feel as calm as the ocean,
And most importantly what is it like to be normal.

Kamilla Legkun (12)
ACS International School, Cobham

Future

Waking up, the shaking I thought was in my head continued,
Slowly opening my eyes all I could see was horror,
The house I once knew was shattered and destroyed,
So ghastly as if I'd fallen into the void,
This void was petrifying, as if outside it hid something horrifying,
Thousands of thoughts wandered around my head,
I went outside instead,
"Am I dead?"
I couldn't feel a thing, despite the chill in the air,
Like the whole world has fallen in despair,
Without a thought of how things could get better,
I only had tears on my sweater.

"How many years has it been!?"
What world am I living in?
The night sky I gazed upon,
Once so quiet,
The symbol of peace,
My childhood flashing before my eyes,
I could hear how the heartbroken night cries,
Had now become a galaxy full of the unknown.
At a glance, it looked like it had been painted, so vivid and bright,
As if there was never a night,
Colours elegantly flowing into the sky hid the actual lie.

"Were these creatures always here?"
"Did the humans disappear?"
Following one wasn't the best plan,
This is where the terror began.

The land we once knew, but disrespect,
Had now taken the effect,
All that was seen was just stone,
And here again I was all alone,
What we did was incorrect,
And now this planet is wrecked.
Boom!
Looking back at that mysterious sky,
I saw that it was time to say goodbye,
This dark but flashing light,
Only filled me with fright.
The creatures knew what was about to happen,
They tilted their heads,
And in a second they were already dead,
Passing the *future* to me to change the outcome of this
foresee.

Waking up everything was blurry,
I guess it was just my worry,
What I had seen was never explained,
But its pitiful image remained.

Nia Delyanova Sarova
ACS International School, Cobham

The End Of The World

I'm just a lonely girl
Watching the world catch fire,
Wishing I'd done what'd been required.

Boom!
There crashed the London Eye
Which we can deny,
But remaining will only be the fire
Even though it's not what we desire.

Smoke attacks my eyes
I cry rivers around me,
My lungs are invaded too,
But what can I do?
Demolished by fire it will all soon be
Leaving nothing to see.

We have no one to blame,
No one but ourselves;
We were warned
Science informed,
Action was necessary
The environment wouldn't cure itself,
No one listened
For it would not affect them,
In a thousand years or more
But not before;

It's too late now
Soon there won't be a world to save
And we have only ourselves to blame;
Consumed by fire,
Because we didn't do what was required.

Weeping clouds
desperately try,
to put out the everlasting fire,
Creating a shield
Leaving the sun concealed,
But it doesn't matter
The memory of it will soon be on fire,
And the weeping clouds can't do what they desire.

Maybe the world will start all over again,
A new beginning
With flowers emerging from the ashes
Shooting out in flashes,
Giving the Earth
A new birth;
Like a tiny streak of light
Shining through a dark night,
But it doesn't matter,
For I -
I'm just a lonely girl
Watching the world catch fire,
Wishing I'd done what'd been required.

Carolina Falkenberg (13)
ACS International School, Cobham

A Grandma She Was

Imagine if you could go back in time
To see family and people dear to you,
My grandma would make a top of my list
All those years from past that flew
Leaving me with an echo of memories that chime.

I could see her gentle, soft smile...
Hear laughter perhaps at a celebration moment
We could be walking down to the beach again,
As without her is like living in torment
The one which seems to last a while...

I could feel her soft skin against mine
For her gentle hugs were the best in the world
The sound of lullabies she sang only for me...
Now I hear them in a distance whilst lying curled
With the power of memories all will be fine.

I picture her life... full of hardship but always with hope,
Rose in the thorns smelling like a bouquet of love
She selflessly gave all that she had
I do hope she sees me from the above,
As being without her is hard for me to cope.

So when I gaze up into the night sky
I recall our happy moments full of fun, joy and bliss,
The laughter we had together skiing Slovenian slopes...

Oh, how I wish I could give her one more kiss!
I do hope my shining star can see me from high...

Imagine if you could go back in time
Who would you spend your time with?
What would you learn, smell, touch or see?
Would you create an exciting life of myth?
Close your eyes and travel back; it is not a crime.

Tia Kenza Scatigna-Gianfagna (13)
ACS International School, Cobham

Remember When You Died?

A bullet hits your skin,
You feel your bones crack.
You fall soon after, and yet,
You feel nothing but the impact.

Swirling black and white,
"Remember death?" the bodies chant.
"Remember when you died?
Why not see if you still can't?"

You cry out.
Darkness drips away, slow but true,
You can see once more, and yet,
A simple soul stands in front of you.

"Remember when you died?
Remember the darkness, or the pain?"
You remember nothing,
Nothing of the sorrow through your veins.

Light fills your vision,
Along with sounds in your ears.
Are you alive?
Your eyes open like they never had in years.

You lift a hand to your chest
And pull it away quickly.
Half-dried blood feels scaly,
As it flows, thick and sickly.

Did you die?
Why did you wake up in the rubble?
It all floods back:
The gunshot
The bullet
The waves of darkness
Black
White
Light

Why didn't you die?

Now what?
Do you try again?
Test the limits of this mortal coil

Until you're lulled back to the dead?

Will you feel the pain?
What if you die?
Will you fall back in the black
Or become an angel up on high?

"Life is meaningless."
The corpses sing their song in the back of your mind.

"Remember when you died?
Remember when you died."

Marion Sky Harper
ACS International School, Cobham

Imagine

Imagine if you lived in a book.
Each day a new page, each week a chapter.

Imagine if your story was told for you.
You have no choice, no opinion than the one written for you.

Imagine if you couldn't stop and think, you just dove in.

Imagine if you could only think, and were too scared to take risks.

Imagine if you were hidden on a shelf nobody looked at.
You collect dust that weighs you down like concrete on your lungs.
If you were a diary, locked up, hidden from the world.

Imagine if you were unfinished, uncertain of what is coming.

Imagine if you were a book, if your story was told for you.

Imagine.

Isabelle Miesner
ACS International School, Cobham

Imagine If The World Was About To End

Imagine if the world was about to end
And the earth started to bend,
And the trees began to fall
And humans became small,
Imagine if the ground roared,
While humans were ignored,

What if I die?
And look up at the sky
And see the destruction we've caused.
Because of us the world is ending,
And now we can stop pretending
That everyone is helping

The pollution
The deforestation
And global warming.
Imagine a bright, black blanket buried on the top of the earth,
Suffocating everything and its worth
And the ground the vibrant colour red

Imagine if the world didn't end
And the world didn't blend

And humans weren't dead
And the ground wasn't red

Imagine if people took care of the world
And tigers weren't poached like the birds,
One day the world will end,
One day the world will end.

Ella Alfakih (12)
ACS International School, Cobham

Heart Of Steel Turned To Gold

Dehydrated, malnourished, and fatigued,
Yet I must go on,
I must keep going.

Every step I take feels like quicksand,
Slowly sinking deeper,
Into the mud and blood of the trenches.

I've never felt so incapable,
Incapable to walk in a straight line,
Incapable to sleep with the sounds of horror that surround
me.

The screams,
Followed by silence,
The gas,
Followed by coughing,
And the gunshots,
Followed by crying.

I've been a crier before,
My heart of steel turned to gold,
And got crushed as easy as paper,
When I saw my friend get shot before my eyes.

I was sitting in a puddle of blood and tears,
But I didn't have time,
Didn't have time to say goodbye,
I needed to leave before a gunshot went through my chest
too.

Jaclyn Lane (13)
ACS International School, Cobham

Imagine If That Could've Happened

Imagine if the meteor had decided to pass?
Would the dinosaurs have lots of sass?
Imagine if they had not built the pyramid?
Would we still have buildings here amid?
Imagine this, imagine that, imagine all of it!

Imagine if sewers weren't invented?
Would we have to have our streets scented?
Imagine if the Greeks had lost the war?
Would we know of Odyseuss' lore?
Imagine this, imagine that, imagine all of it!

History could've changed many a time
Over the course of many lifetimes
History is a half-written book
Things will not change, so look,
write the rest of that half-written book
Imagine this, imagine that, imagine all of it!

Dominic Gavito (13)
ACS International School, Cobham

Imagine

Imagine if there were no stars in the sky,
no one to tell your problems to,
or to tell why your feeling of happiness has suddenly arose
The sky so bland and boring,
with no light or spark to gaze upon
Everyone says the stars used to be so
much brighter than they are now
But how would they know?

Imagine there wasn't any good in the world,
everyone is mean and cruel,
making up excuses to stop themselves from
drowning in their own thoughts
People hating on each other,
not realising the damage they cause
Making it harder and harder for us to maintain
the peace, to spread the love.

Kyla Edwards (14)
ACS International School, Cobham

Imagine

Imagine if the world was empty
Humans no longer there
Imagine if the world was free
Starting to repair

Imagine if the world was green
Animals roamed and grew and thrived
Imagine if the world was healing
Around the world that died

Imagine great green forests
Growing up ahead
Imagine bright blue coral
That used to be dead

I am the few that remember
What the world was like before
When humans trashed the planet
Only plastic on the ocean floor

The world wailed and weeped
While the people ignored
What was rapidly happening
A one-sided war

Alas, they didn't do enough
For with just a puff

Humans without a doubt
Wiped themselves out.

Lucy Grieves (12)
ACS International School, Cobham

The Time I Made History

I made history.
Going through the same misery
Another boring day
The sky still grey
Going to the lab
Taking the same cab
To try the same thing another way

Sitting there thinking
The idea came to me like a bell ringing,
and whispered in my ear
The cure I have been trying to find for a year
And I let out a cheer

Because there it was
The cure to drop the people's jaws
In much worry
Put it to the test in a hurry
Went to tell the group
That I made history in a clear tube

Ran out to see the sky clearing,
and hear all the cheering
This is a victory because,
I made history.

Derin Dengizman (12)
ACS International School, Cobham

The Blizzard

Dusk settles over mountain peak
while clouds scutter in for a restless sleep
the wind whistling a melancholic tune
the thickening snow obscures the moon

the winter winds whipping when you dare to cross its path
throwing snow at exposed faces to show its mighty wrath
the crescendo of the storm beating everyone in its way
as the black flag awakens people are forced to stay

at the rise of the sun, the storm abates
foreboding clouds start to break
the birth of dawn brings hope to the day
as light pierces through, chasing anger away.

Edie Geary (12)
ACS International School, Cobham

A Dream Coming True!

I was studying when *boom*
Some imagines knocked on my door.

Imagine if you become a billionaire
Imagine if you become a successful author
Imagine if you become a famous basketball player

Imagine if all your dreams came true!
It would be like a magical wish for you,
Having a whole new world to explore
A dream you shouldn't ignore

Lying in bed, wishing my dreams shall come true
Closing my eyes, to see a picture
of where I want to be someday.

I dream to become the best version of myself
I dream to never give up.

Victoria Norton Silva (12)
ACS International School, Cobham

We Have No Names

We have no names.
We are the gaps and the empty spaces.
We are the in-between;
The exceptions.

We are the things that scatter in the dark.
We hide away,
Not wanting to be found.
We are the survivors;
The changed and the beaten,
The drowned and the quiet.

Their words haven't faded,
Our wounds haven't healed.
We, the lonely ones,
The wrecked ones,
The starved ones
Have learned to strive,
Invisible, with no identity.

Julieta Garzon-Campos (14)
ACS International School, Cobham

Imagine

Imagine...
Imagine the world stood still
No one outside, humans are ill
And what we so call a mask, is the key
To not getting sick on Christmas Eve
A factor to life is washing our hands
And no passport scans, no flights to the fam
The vaccine will be there the doctors say
Let's hope there's an end to the current way.

Fredrik Muthreich (15)
ACS International School, Cobham

Imagine

Imagine if the world never existed
Imagine if we were never real
Imagine if we were a simulation or a video game
Imagine if the Big Bang never happened
Imagine if happiness was not made
Imagine if we were controlled by technology
Imagine if we were like a dinosaur
Imagine if we couldn't speak
Imagine a world with no illnesses
Imagine if we were dogs and dogs were us
Imagine nobody had legs or arms
Imagine if cars were never invented
Imagine if there was no Christmas
Imagine if animals were not real
Imagine if paper wasn't real
Imagine if we did not have bones
Imagine if we were all deaf
Imagine if there was no light
Imagine if peace was real for once
Imagine if we never had money and you had to steal to live
Imagine if everything was transparent
Imagine if nothing was real, not even space...

Declan Waters (11)
Admiral Lord Nelson School, Portsmouth

Imagine A World Of Kindness

A world of kindness, imagine.
No cruelty, imagine.
No name-calling no more people upset,
But just why?
Why do people have high expectations,
Why can't people think before they speak,
Knowing the impact that their words have,
that makes the other person feel weak?
Why do people have to bring each other down,
Surely the only way is unity and not cruelty?

Imagine a world of togetherness and one,
No discrimination 'cause that's just dumb.
No differences for what's black and what's white.
I'm sorry but why is racism still a thing?
When all of this has all gone and been.
It's the 21st century listen up,
We should all know now when to stop!
Stop the hate and crime 'cause we have had enough,
Everyone deserves to have equal rights,
Without needing to have any fights.

So just imagine,
A world of kindness,
Think about it for a second,
It's a world that I imagine not to be this one,
But to be something you would think is out of the ordinary,
The reason...
Because we wouldn't be used to all the kindness the world
would give us.
So what I'm trying to say is: why can't we make this dream a
reality,
To end all the brutality, and to make what I imagined a
normality.

Raha Mortazaie-Far (13)
Admiral Lord Nelson School, Portsmouth

Imagine If Racism Wasn't A Thing

Imagine if racism wasn't a thing
People wouldn't have to hide away
Because of that quote you said that day

People of all races
Skin colour and or religion
Could feel free to think what they wanted to think

It doesn't matter whether the person is different to you
Or if they follow a different religion to you
You don't say anything about them to anyone

If you do say something to them
They might look okay
But on the inside...

People take things in different ways
People can retaliate or can hide away
People can think, *oh maybe that's true*, and give up

That's not okay

Let people think what they want to think
Let them be who they want to be
Let them believe what they want to believe.

Toby Gilmore (13)
Admiral Lord Nelson School, Portsmouth

Imagine

Imagine, if Jesus was born in June
Imagine, if haters didn't hate
Imagine, if man never walked on the moon
Imagine, if we never had to wait
Imagine, if phones were like a dinosaur

Imagine, if wars were never started
Imagine, if only peace existed
Imagine, if couples never parted
Imagine, if conflict was resisted
Imagine, if life was actually a roller coaster

Imagine, if protesters never protested
Imagine, if words were never spoken
Imagine, if rhymes didn't rhyme
Imagine, if hearts were never broken
Imagine, if racism was never in time.

Imagine, luck was on my side
Imagine, when all is said and done
Imagine, all above being true
Imagine, if this was the poem that won.

Harrison Kimber (11)
Admiral Lord Nelson School, Portsmouth

Imagine The World Without Pronouns

Imagine the world without all the pronouns,
The labels and the names,
Some people don't know what to call themselves,
If you don't know just ask.

Imagine the world without all of the stereotypes,
Girls could like blue without being judged,
Whilst boys could enjoy frilly pink dresses.
Boys would freely wear make-up without the strange glares,
Whilst girls could play football without all the stares.

Imagine the world without all the labels,
Girls could be boys, boys could be girls,
Girls could wear jeans and boys could wear skirts,
They could be who they want to be whatever the day,
If you haven't noticed, times are changing...

Jessica Biggs (12)
Admiral Lord Nelson School, Portsmouth

Imagine

Imagine if everything was free
I get to live my life free
Imagine riding my car down the street
Hah! people will be hearing my beat

Imagine if everything was free
I can have a lot of Xboxes, like three
Imagine gaming all day
Relaxing and keeping things at bay

Imagine if everything was free
I could help everyone like three million and three
Imagine living on the streets
When you can be warm in the nice heat

Imagine if everything was free
What a better place the world would be
A cleaner, brighter better place
Imagine if this were the case

So do just what you want to do and just imagine if this were
true.

Connor Moran-Goodridge (13)
Admiral Lord Nelson School, Portsmouth

Imagine

Imagine a world where you don't feel safe
Imagine a world where you cover your face
6 months inside, feels like a dream
But once you get into it, it causes a scene
Your family are locked away
But here you stay, stay inside that's what they say
Everyone walks around like nothing is happening
When inside your heart is chattering
Your grandparents becoming ill
When your head all of a sudden feels like a grill
In light of the troubles we have today
I have a few things to say
Although the days of this feel long
Together as a country we stand strong.

Amelia Aust (12)
Admiral Lord Nelson School, Portsmouth

Just Imagine

Imagine if the world was free of its cage
Imagine if everyone was set free by the brains
Imagine if COVID-19 happened never
Imagine if we could get rid of all trauma and terror

Just imagine

Imagine a life free of danger
Imagine no one was ever a stranger
Imagine the world was a better place
Imagine that this was just ace

Just imagine

Imagine if all hell broke loose
Imagine we were all struck by Zeus
Imagine peace was completely lost
Imagine everything was just tossed

Just imagine.

Theo Challis (12)
Admiral Lord Nelson School, Portsmouth

Imagine

Imagine if I was taller.
Imagine if I was skinny.
Imagine if I was cooler.
Imagine if I were pretty.

Imagine if I wasn't me.
Imagine if I was popular.
Imagine if you weren't mean.
Imagine I wasn't worth a dollar.

Imagine that you were nice.
Imagine my mum had a job.
Imagine If I could wear Nike.
Imagine I didn't sob.

Imagine you didn't bully me.
Imagine if you didn't say these words.
Imagine if you saw me for who I am; not for who you
wanted me to be.

Chloe Sackett (11)
Admiral Lord Nelson School, Portsmouth

38

Imagine

Imagine if COVID never came around
We would be able to travel without being out of bounds

Imagine if COVID never made us stop
And take in the moments we normally would have forgot
Imagine if covid never made us realise how life can change
at any moment

Imagine if COVID never made us grateful for all the hospital
staff working around the clock
Soon COVID will be cured and we will be free
Again to travel and go to our nan's for a cup of tea

But I-M-A-G-I-N-E if COVID never came around...

Amelia Talbot (12)
Admiral Lord Nelson School, Portsmouth

Imagine If No One Had A Friend

Imagine if no one had a friend,
So lonely and quiet,
No one to lean on or count on,
No one to trust or laugh with,
No one to hug,

Imagine if no one had a friend,
So lonely and quiet,
No one to share your stationery with,
No one to compliment you,
No one to back you up.

Imagine if no one had a friend,
So lonely and quiet,
No one to share memories with,
No one to understand you,
No one to like or love.

How awful the world would be without a friend...

Rosie Powell (11)

Admiral Lord Nelson School, Portsmouth

Imagine Life With No War

There would be no guns.
Or people fighting.
The world would be funner, better.
And there would be less letters.
And less people dying.
And more people are living better.
Other families would not be sad.

Families wouldn't have to reunite with each other.
Less people crying.
Less people hurt.
More family time.
Countries would be at peace.
And they would have a nice life.
Less people would lose their lives.

Imagine if you didn't hear about wars.

Isabelle Veals (12)
Admiral Lord Nelson School, Portsmouth

Imagine if...

Imagine if everyone was the same
The world would be boring
And everyone would go insane
So never try to blend in
Be that person who likes to change
Because if you don't
Your group of friends will be boring
You will be the same
But never act like someone you're not
To blend in
Don't be the chameleon of the group
Show off what you're good at
Tell them about your favourite hat
Don't be someone you're not
Be yourself
Not the chameleon.

Alfie Winter (13)
Admiral Lord Nelson School, Portsmouth

Trapped

Just imagine being trapped underwater
Not able to see your daughter,
Taking your life, in a matter of minutes
30 years old was your life limit

So much opportunity
No more community
You would wish for one more day with your daughter
As you engulf a load of water

Pulled to the ground you take one last breath
Gasping for air
You take one last stare
Remember those times with your daughter
As your eyes come to a close...

Charlie Smith (13)
Admiral Lord Nelson School, Portsmouth

Imagine

Imagine if imagine wasn't a word
And because of your skin colour you were never heard
Imagine if you couldn't talk
And ever since I was born I couldn't walk
Imagine living life in the dirt
Thinking your feelings couldn't be hurt
Imagine if your dreams were sold
Because the shopkeeper thought you were too old
Imagine if you were just trying to lend a hand
Some people would just never understand.

Dylan Keating (11)
Admiral Lord Nelson School, Portsmouth

Crime Time

C rime is the scourge that plagues the city.
R eally think for a second, it is unreasonable, irrational and just uncalled for.
I magine if crime didn't exist.
M aybe life would be great.
E specially for the human race.

T his is where police come in.
I magine if police didn't exist though.
M aybe life would be horrid.
E specially for the human race.

Oliver Emmonds (11)
Admiral Lord Nelson School, Portsmouth

Imagine

Imagine if the world had clear, unpolluted skies
Imagine if 2020 held a good surprise
Imagine if there were no racial remarks
Imagine if kids were allowed fun in parks
Imagine if there was no COVID-19
Imagine if kids could dream
Imagine having a birthday by the stream
Imagine seeing friends and playing tag
Imagine not being in lockdown
Imagine what 2020 could bring
If we all did the right thing.

Lionel Wood (11)
Admiral Lord Nelson School, Portsmouth

Imagine

I magine if children ruled the world,

M aybe we wouldn't have to eat vile veggies,

A lways making your parents go through the hell they put you in,

G etting everything you wanted!

I magine not having to go to school (prison),

N o homework, time doing what you want,

E ducation, however, is important... Maybe it's not the best idea after all.

Madi Pickett (11)
Admiral Lord Nelson School, Portsmouth

Imagine

Imagine if no one was mean
Imagine if we weren't misnamed by bullies or friends
Imagine if racism was gone
Imagine if it was all done

Imagine if we weren't he or she
Imagine if we didn't disagree
With each other or ourselves
Imagine if racism was gone
Imagine if it was all done.

Toby England (11)
Admiral Lord Nelson School, Portsmouth

Imagine

Imagine if the world was free
Imagine if everyone was healthy
Imagine if cancer never happened
Imagine if we could get rid of grief
Only if we believe...

Eleanor Rookley (11)
Admiral Lord Nelson School, Portsmouth

Imagine

Imagine if they could understand,
What it's like to be me.
No more, "Stop crying."
No more, "You're such a geek."

Imagine if they could understand,
What it's like to be me.
No more, "You're so annoying."
No more laughing everywhere I see.

You see,
They don't know me.
They don't know who I really am.
They don't know everything about my life.
They may think they do,
But they are so wrong.
The life of a young carer,
Is far from a cheerful song.

Imagine if they could understand,
What it's like to be me.
No more rolling of eyes.
No more insecurities.

Imagine if they could understand,
What it's like to be me.

No more hatred behind my back.
No more feeling so weak.

You see,
They don't know me.
They don't know who I really am.
They don't know everything about my life.
They may think they do,
But they are so wrong.
The life of a young carer,
Is far from a cheerful song.

So you see,
This world's so judgemental.
But try with all your might,
imagine if you were in my shoes.
What would you find?

A life with no light.

Abigail Fletcher (11)
Bedford High School, Leigh

Imagine If Everyone Was Equal

Imagine, imagine a world where everyone was equal,
No more racist comments,
No more unfair decisions.

Imagine, imagine a world where everyone was equal,
No more deaths,
No more accusations.

Imagine, imagine a world where everyone was equal,
Females get what they deserve,
Many think that this isn't fair.

Imagine, imagine a world where everyone was equal,
This world could change,
And it all starts with you.

Ruby Flanningan (12)
Bedford High School, Leigh

Imagine If You Could See How People Die

Walking down the deep, dark streets
Wondering how someone goes into their fateful sleep.
Tall, small, young and old
Nobody is to be told.
Emotions happy and sad.
Will their death be good or bad?
Babies, adults, elderly, teens,
People questioning how death feels.
What will happen to these poor people?
Falling, hurting, dying, stealing.
How would it feel?

Georgia Marsh (11)
Bedford High School, Leigh

If Only...

I thought it was a dream,
I thought I was the luckiest out there,
It had never occurred to me that my so-called miracle was
actually a forbidden wish,
If only I knew...

The image in my head of the perfect life was now quite
disorientated,
Almost as if it were to haunt my past forever,
It had all begun when the younger me stated,
If only I won the lottery.

And so my wish was miraculously granted,
I personally thought it would've brought me everlasting joy,
And so it did till the delusive love kicked in,
If only, I thought, *I were able to read the intentions of
others.*

And so it happened again,
It was almost as if the universe had it in for me,
The present me still fails to understand why.
Unaware, I was able to do so and was starting to regret my
decisions,
All the negativity had started to get to me,
If only I could escape seconds from the past.

Unsurprisingly, it happened again,
All the fake affection being shown,
Simply for money,
Pathetic.
It had been a week now,
I was unable to plaster a smile on my face,
It felt so hard hiding behind my mask,
It hurt,
If only they could see the sorrow and pain I go through.

I had enough.
Something, someone, or even a force was out there for me,
Everyone left,
Took all I had left,
Forgot about me,
Hated the real me,
Some had even tried to hurt me,
Before their attempt, I solely stated...
If only... I were immortal.

This time I felt victorious,
I smirked,
I had triumph over them,
I won this,
Yet years passed and I was lonely,
I lost this,
I missed company,
I missed being happy,

If only I could go back in history.

Of course I wasn't specific enough,
Only went back a couple of centuries,
I cried,
I realised how badly I messed up, and that happiness isn't all luxury and money,
Yet surrounding people and family,
I sobbed,
I-if only I were free...

To where I awoke.

Aalia Ali
Brampton Manor Academy, East Ham

My Dream World

Do you have a dream?
A dream of peace and harmony,
A world where all children sleep happily,
In a night of silence and peace.
Not a single sound of dreadful planes,
Raiding, to destroy innocent people,
Just for these government wars.

A world of equality,
Where everyone's the same,
Not a single soul irritated about
Race, ethnicity or religion,
Where we can roam the Earth freely,
As brothers and sisters,
In a world of peace and harmony.

A world where all children go to school,
The world glows in happiness and joy,
From their countless, innocent smiles.
A world where children are not needed for work,
In gigantic fields of hard work and terror,
Just for their families to get by.

Everyone has multiple dreams,
But the dream that I have most,
Is a world of peace and harmony,
In a world that I love the most.

Juwairia Iqbal (11)
Brampton Manor Academy, East Ham

A Dream Or A Nightmare?

Hey you, you have some dreams? Don't set them aside!
Let me decide.
Now listen in close
You know I'm no average bloke

A millionaire? How selfish!
All the people who need the money more!
Your friends will leave you for your expensive desires!
You'll turn poor soon anyways.

Live for eternity? Immortality!?
So you want to watch all the people around you die?
Want this giant world all to yourself!
I can't believe it. I'm glad you came to me.

Become a celebrity?
Get caught out. Get cancelled?
Hated by oh so many people.
If you think you would endure it, go on!

Get top grades, fair enough.
But what good will that do? Buy you a house to leave
everyone else alone.
Sure you can get a job, but who will that help?
Nobody but yourself! A selfish one you truly are.

Travel the world!?
You really don't think. The world is already in a bad enough
state.

You want to contribute to that, all the gasses released.
Global warming really won't change for the better with that
goal.

You want to help people? Think you're finally being nice, do
you?
Well, I've got something to tell you. You may help a few, a
hundred.
But there will always be people out there who you'll leave.
You'll betray them while concentrating on one or two
people.

Is that it? Nothing realistic...
How sad, how pathetic you are. Human.
You mortals haven't any sense of selflessness.
It's a pity to see, truly.

Hey, hey you! Don't listen to the demon voice.
Why think so negatively when you can make the right
choice!
You seem to not know... that after all,
If a nightmare can be true, then why not a dream?

Aaliyah Islam (12)
Brampton Manor Academy, East Ham

Many A Dreamer

Dreams,
The very thing people live and die for,
Yet some ignore.

Dreams,
1953
A boy awoke with a dream,
He wanted to change the world,
1963
"I have a dream," that very same boy said
And with those words,
he became a man,
His name: Martin Luther King Jr.

Immortalised in history,
And so are many people like him,
They turned a dream into reality,
Though many stood against them.

Now; you may think,
That you can't,
Because of this and that.

But let me tell you now,
All it takes is courage:

To sacrifice your pride for your dream,
To speak up and have your voice heard,
To sacrifice who you are for who you will become.

Many say they have dreams,
But only a few can call themself dreamers,
They are people who know that,
They may be so prepared yet still fail,
And every time they fail it causes pain, sadness,
disappointment.

But no matter how great the setback
How hard life hits them,
or how severe the failure,
You never give up,
You pick yourself up, you brush yourself off,
You push forward, you move on,
You adapt, you overcome,
That is what I believe.

Dreams,
We all have them,
Only some have enough bravery to turn them into reality,
The question is,
Will you?
Dreams.

Huzaifa Farooqi (12)
Brampton Manor Academy, East Ham

The Perfect World

When you dream of a perfect world,
what pops into your mind?
In my perfect world,
everyone would be kind.

There would be no hatred,
and racism would not exist.
No climate change, no global warming,
and life would truly be bliss.

Discrimination is wrong,
and we all know it's true.
So why do they still get away with it,
leaving people feeling blue?

Don't let them get to you,
don't let them push you down.
Don't let them change you,
don't let them see you frown.

The atmosphere is changing,
filling with CO_2.
Known as global warming,
it leaves us with a cloudy view.

When you dream of a perfect world,
what pops into your mind?

In my perfect world,
everyone would be kind.

Khadijah Munshi (11)
Brampton Manor Academy, East Ham

'Just Imagine'

The universe was dark
God hadn't made his mark
He had many ideas, but which one to choose
Only one could win, the rest would lose

Just imagine
Bins that can walk
Doors that can talk
Books that can read
A cheetah without its speed

Just imagine
An invisible man
Cooking with a fan
A hippo that stings
A harp without its strings

Just imagine
Bears that can fly
A chicken that can say 'hi'
A lion that can't roar
A world without war

Just imagine
Different dimensions
With different inventions

Being able to find your sock
A thief that can't pick a lock

Though God had many choices
He chose our voice
And as long as we have faith
He'll keep us safe.

Irtaza Nayab & Razvan Pocol
Brampton Manor Academy, East Ham

Uncomfortable Rest

Stark, white, cold the clinical room echoed.
Snake-like tubes strapped me in the lonely room
My world which was once large is now narrowed
As I struggled here in this silent tomb

This harsh misery of which I suffer.
From strong to weak, my lifeless figure weeps.
No movement, no control, my brain wonders
This body so frail, it can't be for keeps.

Looks of regret, pity and so much more
Their grief, their horror, their painful distress
My relatives cry, but I must ignore.
I lie in bed, in uncomfortable rest.

But imagine, if we were immortal
Not failing body, enduring crystal.

Dillon Moss (14)
Brighton College, Brighton

The Pressure

Freedom, fun and family running time;
Those were my childhood days of ball sport joy
Then on those pitches I began to shine
Even though we were just a bunch of boys
We were brilliant; we were so sublime
The arrogance of a child's vict'ry game
Even if we wasted a lot of time
Convinced professionals would call my name
But imagine stress, pressure smothering that joy.
Expectations of the country
broken as we lost and missed our one chance
Shame. No longer a pleasurable thing
Crowds thinking why they had wasted money
Coaches watched as they gave a glance askance.

Zach Gari (14)
Brighton College, Brighton

Burial Ground

I am not alone; I am not alone.
The walkway filled with disastrous life.
I had walked away from my solemn home
The sadness plunged into me like a knife
Gone was my happiness and my freedom
Dragged along the vile, horrifying path
Callous words pushed us on, "We don't need 'em."
Death has shown its might and war shown its wrath
Into dreaded, inevitable death
The gas of the German soldiers moves fast
It flows quick through the now death-ridden breath
Its fingers wrapping round my sterile mask
Imagine bright sun breaking through the cloud
Hands reach toward me and then they surround...

Max Dragten (13)
Brighton College, Brighton

A Cure For The Poor

The hospital beds were cursing my head
I lay there with tubes sticking out my gut
I wish someone would just end me with lead
I recall great times I had in my hut
The nurse came by as to tell me the news
It is spreading faster than you can count
It is never good and I always loose
Sometimes I really need to scream and shout out
And yet imagine if there were a cure
I'm still crawling along this dirt-filled floor
In pain I yell out, quietly crying
However, this cure is not for the poor
Because in this mean world money rules all.
Will somebody please stop me from dying?

Edward Stone (13)
Brighton College, Brighton

Competitive Cost

My problems were small when I was younger.
Rounded pebbles, barely enough to scratch,
Mounds in the meadow, amidst the green patch,
Easy hurdles, I was quite a jumper.
Scrambling and laughing and having such fun,
Freedom to run around, every day,
No one forcing you to stop your free play
Soon I'd find I was not the only one...
Imagine the joy, frivolity gone
The eyes of others, harshly critiquing,
Pressured to perform your absolute best
Expectations so high, have to be strong
Got to excel, commentators speaking
Representing your country - what a quest!

Lachlan Mclean (13)
Brighton College, Brighton

The End

Death is calling loudly and taunting me.
I've been toiling, working, desperation
I can't go anymore, this is my plea
No longer energy, no elation
I am getting older, desperate frown
Busyness and pressure and so much stress
My aching muscles, body shutting down.
Creaking bones and throbbing joints - what a mess!
But imagine if you were immortal.
If you could live forever with a gleam.
If death held no pow'r; if there was no pain
Not limited by time of postmortal.
Yet immortality isn't a dream.
Endless eternity stretches again.

Jason Papadopoulos (13)
Brighton College, Brighton

My Darkened World

Can't go outside, filled with anxiety;
I listen in silent acquiescence.
Illness and pain robbed my adolescence,
Why is this such a cruel society?
Doctors said I have melancholia
Quickly put me on antidepressants.
I'm such a wreck. I'm so irrelevant.
Alone, scared, suffering anthrophobia.
But imagine: no, no more depression
If veins could run with hidden elation.
Imagine a world all optimistic,
If I could come out with my confessions,
Out of silence, rid of my damnation.
Could this wish be not so futuristic?

Michael Murphy (13)
Brighton College, Brighton

Imagine Being A Human

Imagine being a human,
selfish, dishonourable, unpredictable,
violent, needy, greedy,
they just want to be the best,
they fight to win or lose and drown,
they will turn your smile upside down.

Imagine being a human,
unworthy, deadly, brutal,
dishonest, corrupt, abrupt,
you can't compete, they'll stoop too low,
they will mangle you up in a neat little bow,
until what was once life, has been turned to strife.

When did we stop being human?
It must have been some time way back,
we destroyed our dignity and ruined our loyalty
now let's sort this out and get back on track.

Imagine being a human,
kind, thoughtful, beautiful,
loving, caring, endearing,
feel it coursing through your veins
as what it means to be human has always been there
now we must strive to stop the pain.

George Pay (14)
Cottingham High School, Cottingham

Imagine...

Imagine feelings could be seen,
A halo, an aura of light that tells us what's within,
A bubble of silver joy as a newborn baby cries.
The grey fog of despair as a loved one dies.

With bitterness and jealousy producing a vile green stench,
Bilious mushroom clouds of orange for duplicity and deceit.
Remorse and regret: a purple haze shading unseeing eyes
And rainbow-faceted, white love shimmering like snowfall.

Anger curdles crimson tides, pouring uncontrollably like lava;
Happiness and excitement: a flurry of yellow petals dancing on the breeze.
The cold depths of a pitch-black shroud of fear,
Never knowing whether to pull or push those we hold dear.

If feelings were visible would we refrain
From the harsh actions and words we do and say?
Would we rejoice in the brightness of another's mood?
Would the warmth of the love they feel break through?

Or would we laugh in the absurdity of others' emotions,
Would we allow them to become a blanketing fog that devours the mind and soul?
Could lying be abolished if it is clear you are deceiving someone?
Would fear be reduced if people can console in clear times of distress?

I can't help but think that if feelings were clear for all to see
People would be kinder, more considerate, there would be
more empathy.
If we saw with our own eyes the effects of words and deeds
Would we strive to do better, would there be more
humanity?

Jacob Gray (14)
Cottingham High School, Cottingham

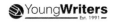

The Hypocrite's Law

There was a room
With glue stuck to the ceiling and tearstains on the desks
And there was a creature
Tapping away at keys, Word document glowing painfully white.
And it wrote its lies.
'We're proud to be a safe community!'
Someone, somewhere, suffered in silent agony;
Their tormentors howled with glee.
'There's always someone to talk to!'
Someone, somewhere, was silent, unheard.
The swarm shrieked empty mottoes and positive quotes.
'Eighty per cent of people feel safe!'
And somewhere
One hundred and eighty doors closed
One hundred and eighty heads bowed
Millions of tears fell.
The creature grinned at a job well done,
Turned to a sea of lifeless faces
And took the register.

Evie Bott (14)
Cottingham High School, Cottingham

End

Doom... Terror... Fright
Thunder crashing... Floods rise
Crimson clouds fill the atmosphere
Earth opens... Mountains shake
Fear
Yet there is a sense of wonder
A calm in the eye of the storm
You know it will come now

You wait
In peace
Full acceptance
No preventing
Deep in thought
You wait
'It will all be over soon'
You sit on the wreckage saying
Crash... Dark... Nothing
Gone.

Ethan Ramsey
Cottingham High School, Cottingham

Escape

Imagine if we ran away
under the stars we could lay
From all of this we would be free
no one else just you and me
I know it sounds like silly dreams
and at this time that's all it seems
But imagine if we ran away
we could be free some day...

Maisy O'Neil (14)
Cottingham High School, Cottingham

Invisible School Days

Slamming the door and the teacher doesn't know what's
going on
Shouting my name in the register but the teacher can't see
me
Pupils are shocked because they can hear me but can't see
me
I can get into mischief inside and outside of school.

It's dinner time and I can get food for free
I can annoy people and they don't know it's me
I keep slamming the doors but they can't see me
I can get into mischief

I don't have to do any work in maths
I hate science but don't have to do any work
I sit next to the teacher but they can't see me
I can get into mischief!

Micky Reynolds (11)
Denton Community College, Denton

Imagine Life Underwater

U nder the sea there's another world.
N ever go beyond the surface.
D on't travel too far down or you might get
E aten by a shark!
R ed lobsters with big red eyes scuttle by.
W ater crashes against the rocks.
A ll the fish swim smoothly through
T he waving water.
E very day I hear the sharks growling and shouting as they
R ide across that waves.

Marko Gotovac (11)
Denton Community College, Denton

The Invisible Helper

Imagine if I were invisible
I would make dreams come true
By helping humans and their animals too.

I would sneak into their house
And make sure everyone was happy
And make sure the baby was in a clean nappy!

I would put presents under the tree,
For everyone to see
How lovely Christmas could be.
All thanks to invisible me!

Ruby Hill (11)
Denton Community College, Denton

Imagine If The World Was A Sweet Shop

Over the hills and over the grass lies
Sweets shining like stars
Getting brighter and brighter.
The grass is so soft, like I am walking on clouds.

Sweets were shining in my eyes.
My mouth couldn't stop watering.
I dashed and grabbed some sweets.
It felt like heaven.

Kaitlyn McCormack (11)
Denton Community College, Denton

Imagine

Sometimes, even though people are surrounding me,
I still feel like I'm going to be lonely forever.
I feel like I'm in a pit
I am unable to climb out.
I try all the time
But it feels like
People keep dragging me back
Down.
Down
To the place I hate the most.

Ava Lynch (12)
Denton Community College, Denton

Imagine Gameworld

G ames are real
A ll the people are controlled
M any people but
E veryone is equal.
W hen it starts they drive fast
O ver the pixel bridge
R acing about
L oudly
D etermined.

Cody Tunnicliffe (11)
Denton Community College, Denton

Dream Life

M ight have an adventure
Y ou're welcome to join

D reams come true
R eality doesn't exist
E very day is different
A re they real?
M ayhem!

Skye Kay (12)
Denton Community College, Denton

Superpowers

P owers could be so helpful!
O verpowered you could be
W e all could fly anywhere
E very day would be an adventure
R eal-life with real powers
S o cool!

Luke Jones (11)
Denton Community College, Denton

If I Was Immortal

The joy of jumping off the bridge,
Watching my friends all perish.
As I have a secret none of them knew,
I am immortal through and through.

I would explore the world,
Watching exotic dancers spin and twirl.
I would invade the dangerous tribes,
And make it out with my everlasting life.

I would go on dangerous adventures with my friends
Hoping they'd come to a deadly and gruesome end
You see I had done all the fun I could do
So I took up murdering as time went through.

But eventually this all came to an end
As global warming took a bend
People in factories tried to help
But instead they made the Earth yelp
They left the nuclear factories hoping they would go
But they watched as the factories imploded.

Thanks, factory workers, now I'm here
Floating the space, oh dear.
Time should go on, oh this will be long.
I wish I wasn't immortal, I wish I could die
Well, at least now I can fly.

Victoria Cross (12)
Dyson Perrins CE Academy, Malvern

Imagine If You Were Them

This is odd, this is strange,
I'm not quite sure I like this change
Wait no, what am I saying?
This is the thing for which I've been praying
The perfect hair, the perfect skin
And also I'm extremely thin.

Hey is that the old me over there
Sitting alone on that little chair?
Look at all those ugly clothes
People taking pictures of me on their phones

Oh look! The test results have been posted
A failure party my friends will have hosted
Looky there I got a three
That was a for sure guarantee
But what did old me get I wonder?
Perhaps I'll go and confront her
Never mind I can see
Hold up, she got a ninety-three!
Oh yeah, I used to be pretty smart
Perhaps I wasn't right to depart

At least my clothes were pretty comfy
I miss that I was awkwardly clumsy

And also I was pretty intelligent
I think that's become pretty evident
Although I have been having a ball
Was this the right thing to do after all?

Cindy-Louise McNally (12)

Dyson Perrins CE Academy, Malvern

Imagine If I Had One Wish

Imagine if I had one wish
Anything could be mine in a swish
What could I wish for? So many choices
I could speak over so many voices
Maybe I should save it
Better not brave it
I'll just get on my way to school
If they hear about my wish, certainly they'll drool
"Megan, Megan!" says my best friend.
Did they find out? Is this the end?
"Did you revise for the test? I did it in the bath."
A test? A test? Are you having a laugh?
I don't wanna be here, I'd rather be in a zoo
Oh gosh, oh gosh! Whatever shall I do?
For this is the test I surely have dread
Oh no, I sure wish I was dead!

Megan Kimber (12)

Dyson Perrins CE Academy, Malvern

Global Warming

G reenhouse gases fill the air
L eaves brown and decayed
O il leaking into rivers and streams
B urning fossils to fuel our cars
A nimals are all gone
L ong gone

W ater is black and diseased
A cids running through the pipes
R otting food in abandoned homes
M onoxide gas engulfing the streets
I t's a dark place out there
N othing is left, everything dead, the
G overnment turned a blind eye, now look what happened.

Danielle Cochrane (13)
Dyson Perrins CE Academy, Malvern

Imagine If There Was No School

I really don't like school
Whoever likes it I think they're a fool
School dinners, they smell out of date
I always get into trouble just because I'm late.
Maths is boring
I end up bored and snoring.
The English teacher says I don't know my punctuation.
While I'm waiting for my graduation
History is learning about the past while I want to get out of there really, really fast.
Drama is always about the act.
But it's just plain old facts
Geography means learning about plants
The teacher always says, "Have you got ants in your pants?"
You'd think art is fine
But it's actually about shapes and lines.
RE is definitely the worst
But if there was a boring contest it would be 1st
PSHE is about your health
But after 24 seconds you'll start to belch.
Science, you'd think it's fun
But once your in there you'd want to run
Computing you'd think it's fun and games
But you'll soon find out it's really lame

Language you learn new stuff
But it's actually really rough
PE is running around,
And you'll find your stuff in the lost and found.
That's my timetable
I know, I know it sounds like a fable!

Abdullah Patel (11)
Eden Boys' School, Preston

Imagine

Imagine
Imagine that you are the last person on Earth
Imagine that there is no food
Nothing
Your stomach explodes with anger
There is nothing for you to do
Imagine
Imagine that it's just rubbish, rubble and wildfires
Nothing to stop it
An abandoned world
Imagine
Imagine that you go mad in this lifeless world
Lost in a black darkness and sadness forever
Imagine
Imagine that you could do anything you want
Anything
But you will be alone by yourself
Imagine
Imagine what will happen when this comes true
Well
We're already heading towards it
So let's make it change
We can change this together

But
Not
Alone.

Abdur-Rahman Wadie (11)
Eden Boys' School, Preston

Imagine

Imagine if you could detect lies,
the person who you thought was your best friend,
and the people who were thought to be your family,
you find out who they really are...
They lie to you and you see a red light,
and you know what it is,
you go to school and see who you thought was
your best friend, you ask him to say his name,
the red light flashes,
the lie is detected...
If it who could it be,
you run back home,
your parents say son,
light goes beep,
once again lied to who even are they,
once a home how a nightmare,
where do I go,
lied to again,
not even school is a safe place,
where do I go,
after being lied to again...

Aamir Motala (12)

Eden Boys' School, Preston

Imagine

Flying high up in the sky,
with sails reflecting light.
We saw it from over the house,
it looked as small as a mouse.
We ran to keep an eye on it,
and we saw it dive into a cave.
As we peeked to get a glimpse,
we saw it shred a sheep.
Before smoking it with its heat,
we looked at it in awe!
Talons sharper than knives,
and horns swirled in pride.
Its tail was long and scaly,
while fangs short but sharp.
This is the thing we saw,
when it lifted its head and roared.
It took off into the sky,
with wings cutting through the air.
What was it?

Ibraheem Bhula

Eden Boys' School, Preston

Imagine If...

Imagine if you could
see what I see.
Imagine if you can
think like me.
Imagine if you could
be me.
Imagine if you knew
the real me.
Imagine if you knew the
real you.
Imagine if you could know
what people were thinking.
Imagine if someone could
see you...
the real
you.
Imagine if you could
see through walls.
Imagine if you
were me.
Under my shoes.
Under my suit.
Under the mask...

This is the real me.

Mohammed Rayan Zafar (12)

Eden Boys' School, Preston

Imagine I Am A Superhero

I can fly in the sky
and I can defeat villains,
when I am chilling.
I can run at a fast speed
to do a good deed.
I am strong
I could kill King Kong
I can take the form of an animal,
mostly mammals.
I am a hero
and the villains are zero.

Aahil Chughtai (11)

Eden Boys' School, Preston

Imagine

If I had good memory
I would be king
My heart would sing
If I could beat people in the ring
My heart would sing
If I had power over the world
I would be king
If I could fly
People ask why
I would rule the world
If I could live without fear
I would rule the world.

Fazale Subhan (11)
Eden Boys' School, Preston

Imagine If They Knew The Real You

Imagine if they knew the real you; the one you constantly hide
What if they actually knew and felt the continuous pain we go through.
The mask we use to cover up the pain, until we feel safe.
Imagine if we could change pain we go through.
All our sorrows and pain would be lost for all we know.
We desire to feel complete; where do we start?
We fill our lives with places and things and never think of the people who worry.
We aspire to be people we think are perfect.

But are they really perfect under all that make-up and false veneer?
Midnight, is where we cry for all we have lost.
We try to remember the power we have over our pain.
But we don't realise the pain that all our friends go through when they are in trouble.
We don't understand the stress our carers and parents go through in helping us.
When we push people away when we need them most.
The chaos we cause when we blurt out our destructive feelings to everyone.
We hide how we really feel: desperate to be understood.

Ekjyot Bhambra (14)
Exhall Grange School, Ash Green

Imagine

Imagine if I was a K-pop star,
I was on the stage.
I would write lots,
of songs and albums.
One day I would have dance practice,
Like once a week.
Imagine if I was a K-pop star.

Imagine if I was a K-pop star.
I would have a big house
with lots of bedrooms.
I would go out shopping
with my staff,
So I wasn't alone.
Imagine if I was a K-pop star.

Imagine if I was a K-pop star.
I was in a luxury hotel.
I would go to the stadium to rehearse,
My dance moves while
singing as well.
Imagine if I was a K-pop star.

Imagine if I was a K-pop star.
I was performing to my army fans,
All over the world.

After my performance I would go back to,
The luxury hotel.
Imagine if I was a K-pop star.

Imagine if I was a K-pop star.
After my performance in England,
I would go to the car then to the airport.
I would go on my private jet to America,
for my tour.
When I arrived I would go to the hotel.
Imagine if I was a K-pop star.

Imagine if I was a K-pop star.
I would go to my hotel room.
In my hotel room I would unpack my luggage,
While I was on tour in America.
Imagine if I was a K-pop star.

Imagine if I was a K-pop star.
I would get changed backstage before my performance.
After I got changed I would wait by the lift step.
When I was on stage I would see my army,
of fans on the screen.
Imagine if I was a K-pop star.

Imagine if I was a K-pop star
I would start my performance for my fans.
When the backing track was playing,
I would sing along with the track.
Imagine if I was a K-pop star.

Joshua Powis (12)
Exhall Grange School, Ash Green

Imagine If You See A Ghost Girl...

Imagine if the night is dull and dark,
And you are heading past a park,
You hear a noise sounding like whimpering,
So you go and see where it is lingering,
It sounds like a girl, she is crying, you hear it loud and clear,
That's when you realise that she must be near,
You dash around, yelling, "Who is there?"
You finally find her but the sight of her you cannot bear,
"Who is this filthy wretch?" you declare,
For what you see, you are ill-prepared,
She is in a gown, tattered and filthy,
Her hair is brown, lustrous and silky,
She is on a swing moving ever so slightly,
Then she stands up with her fists clenched tightly,
You cannot see her eyes for they are obscured by her fringe,
She reveals them slowly which makes you cringe,
They are black, nothing more, nothing less,
You have never seen anyone like her, she is such a mess,
Suddenly, your eyes become fixed to her eyes,
Somehow this makes you want to cry,
You feel ever so ill, are you going to die?
Tears start to run down her pale white cheeks,
You have no control over your body so your eyes, too, begin to leak,

Imagine if this nightmare did indeed come true,
Let's just hope it never happens to you...

Amelia Smith (13)
Exhall Grange School, Ash Green

Imagine If You Won The Lottery

Oh joy of joys!
You will never believe this!
10,000 pounds all for me!
I won it with luck on my side,
That lottery ticket has changed my life

I'm going to spend it on things I never dreamed of
Like sports cars, huge mansions and bottles of champagne
But I have to spend it on unimportant things too
Like bank cheques and taxes
Oh! Those things are a pain!

Then, bit by bit, all my money is going
Note after note, they teleport into the cash register
And all they give me is a measly one pound coin
What is that even worth? You must be joking.

My family keep asking to lend them cash
"No!" I shoot back. "This money's for me!"
Then the bank ask for the monthly payment by email
I never reply
Then it's all a memory
My cash has all gone in a whirlwind

Thanks to my selfishness, my family and those who I hold so dear
Have shut me out of their lives
Curse this lottery ticket!
I wish I had never won, I wish I was never rich
I wish that my family would let me in
I wish
That I was me again.

Lucy Rees (13)
Exhall Grange School, Ash Green

Imagine If Dreams Were Real...

Imagine if dreams were real,
Fairies and unicorns, glitter and gold,
Castles, foreign lands and picturesque places,
Dreaming, dreaming, again and again...

Big, gleaming towers and epic tales,
Tales that actually come to life,
Amazing adventures, overcoming adversity,
Dreaming, dreaming, again and again...

Pirates, treasure and grand ships at sea,
Birds and mythical creatures flying high in the sky,
Wonder and amazement spreading from your head to your toes,
Dreaming, dreaming, again and again...

If you had one wish, what would it be?
To live in an opulent castle or a hut by the sea?
You could see back in time or ahead to the future
Dreaming, dreaming, again and again...

You could be an inventor devising new creations,
Own your own farm, be at one with the land,
Connect with the pet you have always wanted
Dreaming, dreaming, again and again...

Sumptuous chocolates wrapped in gold,
A brand-new house to behold,
All these dreams could come true,
It really is just up to you.

Kyla Lawrence (13)
Exhall Grange School, Ash Green

Imagine If...

Imagine if,
you could do anything!
From cooking anything,
to a multi-world champion,
in every sport possible!

You would have,
multi-millions,
of rewards and,
over a,
trillion dollars!

Top of,
the tables,
more wins,
than Hamilton!

Have visited,
every single,
country in,
the world!

Have the most,
wins in every,
single,
videogame.

Are the,
most popular,
in school

More money,
than,
Bill Gates!

More subs,
than,
T-Series!

Broke every,
single world,
record possible!

Highest IQ,
of anyone!

You know,
everything!

You've been,
everywhere!

Wake up!

George Williams (14)
Exhall Grange School, Ash Green

If There Was No Up Nor Down

What if people and animals could walk up walls?
Then what would up or down be?
Then you'd find the only implication of up or down is when you'd fall.
Up is above. Down is below.
Direction is an illusion.
Direction is a lie.
Direction is a matter of perspective.
What if people and animals could walk up walls?
How would this affect evolution?
What's the point of flying when you could sprint up a building without gravity holding you back?
Maybe flightless birds would be more common.
Or would the air be a place to escape predators?
What if people and animals could walk up walls?
How would this affect architecture?
We wouldn't need, stairs, ladders, escalators, ramps, lifts or any other mechanisms.
If there was no up nor down, where would the roof be?
Just imagine. What if?

Nathan Field (14)
Exhall Grange School, Ash Green

Imagine

Imagine if you could stop suffering forever...

S adness would stop
T o be happy
O utrage would come to an end
P overty would end

S ickness stops
U pset would be in the past
F amine would be over
F loods would be a rainbow instead
E arthquakes would end
R ich and the poor would be equal
I gnorance would be stamped out
N ow you are your own person
G rief-stricken would be happy

F orest fires would be a thing of the past
O ld pain would become new happiness
R acism would become old news
E quality would be a thing
V olcanoes would stop forever
E verything would be accepted
R udeness would be ignored.

Grace Wheeler (12)
Exhall Grange School, Ash Green

Imagine If...

On the most luxurious of mats,
Or on the comfiest of laps,
Or got to chase rats
Whilst wearing top hats.

Imagine if dogs couldn't smell...
The police would never tell
What the criminal would usually sell,
To his common customer Mel.

Imagine if rats didn't have a tail
And if instead, monkeys got mail
Or if it didn't exist, the one we call snail.
Now surely that'd be odd without fail
Especially if penguins could sail.

Imagine if humans could never say hi
Or if elephants wore a tie.
Imagine if antelope were told the end is nigh,
Whilst it was actually just a terrifying lie.

Imagine if animals were sexist...
Or maybe didn't ever exist...

Imagine if animals couldn't do what they normally do!

Lucy Hibbert (14)
Exhall Grange School, Ash Green

Imagine If Monsters Ruled The Night

The streets are crawling with monsters every night.
You hear creepy sounds,
Afraid in case a monster breaks into your house.
You and try to protect yourself.

You're hiding in a dark, scary room
Then you hear a sudden noise
Of something smashing to the ground.
You go and search for what it was.

All of a sudden the wind starts howling
You catch sight of it... The monster king!
Standing right in front of you. He has a black body,
White eyes and sharp teeth that are as yellow as the sun.

You find something to protect yourself with.
You and the monster king fight.
A colossal fight to the end.
You defeat him.

Suddenly you awake... turn around.
There is no monster to be found.

Cian Orme (11)
Exhall Grange School, Ash Green

Imagine If You Were In The War

Imagine the pain, the blood, the suffering.
Imagine the loss, the memories.
Imagine the things you'd see, hear, smell.
Imagine the rapid rattle of those guns.
The dropping of the bombshells.
The field of corpses that lay before you...
Imagine the silence, the peace and quiet, the victory in the war.
And then, nothing.
Like time stops around you, like your whole world has changed.
You lie there.
Lying in your bed like nothing happened.
Like it was all a dream, in your imagination perhaps.
Everything you saw, everything you felt. It's all gone...

Daniel Bugg (14)
Exhall Grange School, Ash Green

Imagine If We Were All Equal

No fights would take place at all,
No wars would be happening,
The countries would live in peace and prosperity,
Dreaming that there would be,
No racist comments,
Just because they're black or white,
Doesn't mean they deserve comments that are offensive,
Imagine,
Lots of respect for the disabled,
Young or old,
But sometimes what we imagine in our minds
Won't come true like we want it to,
What we can do,
Is try our hardest,
Be the best we can be,
Just imagine in your minds today,
If everyone was treated equally.

Lainey Milligan (13)
Exhall Grange School, Ash Green

Imagine Being A Character In A Computer Game...

Imagine if we were just avatars in a computer game passively waiting for the humans to direct us.
Hear the thundering footsteps, the money drops into the machine,
the click of the controller... 1, 2, 3...
Accessing the game.
We wait for something to happen.
The command is activated. We perform.
Running for our lives, jumping platforms, avoiding snakes, explosions and Fighting back against the enemy.
Game over... Exhausted... Our job is done.

Sophie McNally (15)

Exhall Grange School, Ash Green

Imagine If...

Z   ombies ruled the world

O   nly Death roamed.

M   ayhem infected and spread everywhere, walking in flesh.

B   ecoming one of them was like fearing the end.

I   magine seeing one of them in front of you, they'd get you at any second.

E   ven hearing them... It would give you chills down your spine.

S   earching the world in hiding, trying to live until the zombies go again. A mad time indeed.

Lexie Todd (11)
Exhall Grange School, Ash Green

If I Was Invisible...

If I was invisible,
Finally I could hide.
Indestructible to everything
Walking through walls.
All the candy I could steal!
Spy on the rest of the world.
In a world of my own
Nowhere to be seen.
Vengeance could be mine.
I could save the world.
See people who can't see me.
Interfere in world problems.
Be a ghost and scare people.
Let myself escape from the rest
Of the crowd.
Most importantly I could
End world suffering.

Kirath Mann (11)
Exhall Grange School, Ash Green

Imagine If You Were Here...

Imagine if you could see the rolling hills and towering trees,
You could hear the river flowing gently by,
You could smell the forest flowers and morning dew,
You could feel the gentle breeze and warming sun,
Imagine you could hear the birds singing in the light of dawn,
You could see the deer grazing peacefully in the fields,
Imagine if you were here.

Tyla Basra (13)
Exhall Grange School, Ash Green

Imagine

If I was an elf.
A fabulous worker for Santa.
Speedily wrapping presents for boys and girls.
Watching to see if they're behaving themselves.
Always on standby for Santa's next job.
Snow falling on the ground.
Away to the sleigh with a bag load of presents.
Load up the reindeers and we're off!

Maximus Warwood (12)
Exhall Grange School, Ash Green

Imagine If I Met God...

If I met God
I would talk to God a lot
We would sit on clouds
Just God and I.

I cannot see him
But I know he can see me
I would pray to him to put the world right.
Stop pandemics, plastic pollution
And put a stop to global warming!

Harry Rawden (11)
Exhall Grange School, Ash Green

A World Without Bird Song

Imagine a world without birdsong,
Our days would be bleak and long,
Something that we take for granted,
That seems to be implanted,
In our world forever,
But what if we were to never,
Hear this sweet tune,
Only to be encrypted in a rune,
The mystery voice which keeps you company,
Irreplaceable with money,
Yet why do we ignore,
The song from the moor?
Possessed by technology,
Birdsong might as well be mythology,
Crisp and sweet in the morning,
Have you forgotten your friend?
Who kept you sane while soaring,
Closer to the end,
Our world is dying,
Yet you keep denying,
If I could change it all,
I'd go back to the start,
Back to when humans had a heart,

Back to when nature played a role,
Before humans used coal,
Back to when birdsong was a gift,
Through history I sift,
When did we ease to appreciate?
When did we build a gate?
Dividing us, breaking the bond,
No longer as fond,
As we were before,
Now with a virus we are at war,
Simple yet moving,
One day we will be rueing,
The day we didn't listen,
So can't we strive,
To enjoy the simple yet complex things in life?

Marika Wasikiewicz (11)

Fitzharrys School, Abingdon

Imagine If This Poem Is Your Reality

Imagine if you couldn't go to school,
Imagine if you were trapped in an enchanted cage where you couldn't see anyone,
Imagine if your life was at risk because you saw your family,
But what if you couldn't go to school because of a global pandemic?
And what if that enchanted cage you were trapped in was your own house?
Maybe you caught the deadly virus just by seeing your family?
Imagine if this poem you are reading is your reality!

Daniella Jones (12)
Fitzharrys School, Abingdon

Imagine: If Everyone Was Equal

If everyone was equal,
If there was no rich or poor,
If no one was bullied,
If no one cared how they looked,
If everyone could see they were special and unique,
This world would be perfect.
No pollution and no crying from hunger,
No poverty,
A world filled with love,
A world where you can go for a walk under the night sky
without being filled with fear,

A peaceful world,
A world where hopes and dreams would come true,
A world where everyone worked together,
A world where dangers were extinct,
A world where everyone was treated the same, no matter
the colour of their skin, gender or even religion.
A perfect world,
A world where everyone was equal.

Laura Ferreira de Oliveira (13)
Great Academy Ashton, Ashton-Under-Lyne

If Humans Went Extinct

If humans went extinct,
What would it be like?
One could think it'd all be bad,
But Earth would surely thrive,
There would be no increases in pollution,
Or anything that harms the Earth.

Mother Earth's creatures could live,
Without fear of being abused,
Nor would they be manipulated,
For what some call entertainment.

Humans are really a twisted species,
Our deaths would not matter.
If you really think about it,
We made Planet Earth suffer,
For our own gain.
Her killing us all off,
Would be her own way of revenge.

If humans went extinct,
Would it really be all that bad?
If we can't save Earth,
From something our elders caused,
Could we still call ourselves advanced?

It'd be our own fault,
If we were to go extinct.
Think of it as payback,
For destroying our planet,
And making a world where younger generations would suffer.

To the older generations,
Think of it as payback,
You ruined the lives of children,
Before they were even born.
So, what if you didn't know what you caused?
That's no excuse for making them suffer.

If humans went extinct,
Earth could be at rest.
No more pain for her,
If we took our final breaths.

Elisha Richards (13)
Great Academy Ashton, Ashton-Under-Lyne

Imagine A World

Imagine a world much greater than ours
A world where smiling flowers grow
With no thorns to wound our golden hearts
Where life is turned into a flower
And spreads its gentle fragrance around our broken Earth

Imagine a world where children play freely
Parents' eyes are filled with the joy of their youngsters
A new world without fear and pain
No cries, no poverty and no tears

A world where everyone has someone
None are abused and not a single hand is unclean
Where not a soul is injured
And everyone lives with love and harmony
A world much different to ours
Yet the same in many ways

Imagine a world where anything is possible
Where dreams come true
And people are supporters not enemies
And believers live amongst dreamers
And there is equal dignity

Imagine our lives dancing like the rain
Twisting, twirling, turning
Endlessly with delight

With nothing to fear
And no one to hate

Imagine the impossible because it may be possible...

Imaan Ahsan (13)
Great Academy Ashton, Ashton-Under-Lyne

Imagine

Imagine if no one was sad,
Only if the world wasn't that bad,
If people knew how words cut deep,
Words we think about when we go to sleep.
Imagine if everybody knew,
What every person is going through,
If everyone would help you out,
Especially when you are in doubt.
Imagine if the world wasn't cruel,
Only if people weren't used as tools,
If everyone was appreciated,
Just valued - not depreciated.
Imagine if every sickness had a cure,
To help the people who are pure,
If only the world was perfect,
Then everyone would have respect.
Imagine if everyone were their best,
Maybe this world wouldn't be in a mess.

Skyler Shaw (13)
Great Academy Ashton, Ashton-Under-Lyne

Imagine

Imagine if you had nobody
Nobody to talk to
Nobody to play with
Nobody to laugh with
Imagine if you were going through a tough time
But there was no one to make you laugh
It was like drowning and having no one to help you
Imagine being submerged in your own thoughts
And you couldn't express them to anyone
Imagine if you needed comfort
But there was nobody to hug you
Having nobody is reality for some people
So we should be grateful for what we have.

Vidhi Shah (13)
Great Academy Ashton, Ashton-Under-Lyne

Imagine

Imagine you were them,
You were quite popular,
But once there was an event,
Even though people thought you were irregular,
You dreamt a dream,
A dream that was not so much a dream more a beginning,
You came up with a scheme,
It was so thrilling,
You were who you wanted to be,
People knew who you were,
They knew your name but not your story unmistakably,
Your head was in a whirl,
They had no idea, what if they did,
Imagine if they did...

Olivia Hayhurst (12)
Great Academy Ashton, Ashton-Under-Lyne

The Power Of Imagination

Imagine if we could travel in time,
Discover the mountains that we will climb,
Looking back at history,
And moving forward to see our destiny.

Imagine if our hopes were fulfilled,
All would be exceedingly thrilled,
Our wildest dreams could come true,
The day we would all be smiling through.

Imagine if we were not seen,
And nobody knew where we had been,
To be invisible for just a short while,
On our faces would be an unseen smile.

Zulaykha Sheikh (12)
Great Academy Ashton, Ashton-Under-Lyne

Imagine If Everyone Had One Wish...

Imagine you had one wish
Would everyone be happy?
Or would the world become...
Disasterous?

Would that wish change you
For the *better* or *worse?*

Imagine your wish made you happy
But not others.
Your wish *hurt* the only person you *loved*

Imagine you had a second wish.
This wish made everyone *happy.*

Afsana Siddiqa (13)
Great Academy Ashton, Ashton-Under-Lyne

Imagine

You brought the family together,
You were here with us,
And were always there for us,
You'll always be in our heart.

Everyone thinks about you,
As if you were always there,
You were an amazing grandparent to me, Millie and Henry,
You'll always be in our heart.

Why did God choose you to be an angel?
But you can always watch down on us,
You'll always be in our hearts.

God has chosen the right angel,
He will give you an incredible life up in Heaven,
You'll always be in our hearts.

You will be the biggest part of the family for many years to come,
And me myself, Maisy Montgomery, is proud to be your great-granddaughter,
You still bring a smile to me and others,
And will always be in our hearts!

Maisy Montgomery (11)
Guilsborough Academy, Guilsborough

Once The Wind Blew

Once the wind blew, fresh as can be,
The grass was lush, it felt good to be me,
The ocean was new, filled with life,
The night was filled with stars, so bright,
Foxes and deer prance around,
The mice scuttled with no sound.

I climbed dwarf mountains,
Putting the stone on the pile,
I was finally free!
I walked down with a smile.
And that was the day I realised that nature is so much more,
Than trees, grass and the ocean's shore.
But now it's polluted, filled with dust
Litter flying everywhere from dawn til' dusk
There is no more life left in the sea,
And no more room for me to be me.

Now the sea is plastic,
It covers it thick,
Where will the animals live?
The question makes me sick.
When will you realise that this is wrong,
Because the lovebirds can't sing their song.

True the wind does blow,
The grass was lush, and when it snows,
The ocean is brown with no life,
And the hunters causing all their strife,

No more deer prancing around,
And no more wildlife making their sound.
Will I see the sunset again?
Or will there be no more girls or men?
Will the mountains grow and grow?
And the world will be polluted and will it stop, no!
Not until we clean it up so...

Once the wind blew fresh as can be,
Why won't anyone listen to me?
Does anyone realise that,
The world has changed,
And that's a fact!

Amelia-Rose Montgomery (12)
Guilsborough Academy, Guilsborough

Imagine

What if you and your soulmate were joined with a single piece of thread
The thread could be thousands of miles long, carefully wrapped around your finger, a beautiful shade of pink, blue or red.
It could stretch from London to Hong Kong. You pull it further towards you,
It might feel weird to be attached to someone unknown but your soulmate comes closer by an inch or two stopping you from feeling so alone.
The only problem with this perfect fairy tale would be if the thread were to break.
It is the unfortunate flawed detail of a world that could be filled with love that isn't fake. If you were to finally meet, you would feel loved, not neglected.
Together forever, and always perfectly connected.

Maisie Given (14)

Guilsborough Academy, Guilsborough

Just Imagine

Just imagine if you lived a different life
Where the sky was red and the clouds were blue
Your parents were your siblings
Or your brother was your dad and your sister your mum

Just imagine you being a completely different person
You could've even been a person who was angry all the time
Or someone with no feelings at all
You could've been someone that didn't know what was right
and what was wrong

Just imagine everyone in the world hating you
Or everyone in the world loving you so much you just
explode
You could've had all your anger or excitement bottled up
'Cause you were scared what people were going to think of
you

Just imagine not being you...

Brooke Dibra (12)
Guilsborough Academy, Guilsborough

Imagine

Here we are as yet still beating steady
I hear our voices in the whispered wind.
Our hollow flame burns our bodies ready,
Whilst empty flesh crowds eyes expressly dimmed.
What of love? Plaintive pain of life's deceits,
These fires rage about us and beyond us,
I hear the murmurs of these twisted sheets
Whilst words congeal and blood is binded thus.
There is yet the smoky haze of winter,
As though to signal truth is truly lost
O' and berries dream and branches splinter,
So simply: nothing breaks this dizzy frost.
And yet I hear the blackbird sing his song,
As though this love were real and we were wrong.

Hannah Tilt (15)
Guilsborough Academy, Guilsborough

Hyenas

I am trapped, darkness closing in on me,
The tap, tap, tap of your words on the screen,
Wishing you would go away, let me be,
Silently suffering, don't make a scene.

But again and again, you come, hungry
And howling like hyenas, no escape,
Frozen with fear when I want to run free,
Each day, I'm shadowed by your looming shape.

Staying home will not help. I taste the blood
From my wounds as you cut deeper, breaking
Down my walls, will death save me, make life good?
Piercing words break through, leaving me shaking.

I nearly jumped but her voice was so kind,
She saved me, assured me, healed my mind.

Katie Nicholls (13)
Guilsborough Academy, Guilsborough

Imagine

Every train travels by railroad or tracks,
And the ageing mind is prone to vestige
When humans are but tamed animals in packs.
Before, this was much their simple life.
But when undenied fear begins to pool
Will then your love only delays this fear?
With many kids having to leave their school,
Down a cheek dismally drips a lone tear,
As many more are displayed to torture.
Guns are ablaze, many have claimed shots.
Million a soldier seen as amateur.
Finally the crestfallen crying stops.
The terrible world war has now ended,
Yet broken hearts will never be mended.

Oliver Green (14)
Guilsborough Academy, Guilsborough

God

If God knows everything there is to know
then I ask how can God learn or grow
if you knew all that was and all that will be
then how will your decisions you make be free?
If you were everything and everything was you
then there would be nothing for you to do
and then we find gold in this very position
imprisoned by the power for him to keep was his decision
and so God created a place of limitation
that confusing place we call creation
Most people pray
Whereas others believe that the lord is nothing but a myth
till this day.

Yuvraj Singh (12)
Guilsborough Academy, Guilsborough

Through My Eye

Through my eye you could see another world,
One that's been waiting for me to find out,
Through the mirror on the wall,
There's a life for me to spare,
One that's great and one that's fun,
One for life that would never end,
One I can trust, one I can love,
Through the eye of my love.

Ashley Prickett (11)
Guilsborough Academy, Guilsborough

Imagine If Africa Was Not Colonised

How we would be so rich,
And never end up in a ditch.

We would rule like queens and kings,
And show the world our bling.

There would be no more racism,
But we would have lots of tourism.

We would have many stable civilisations,
Without the colonisation.

Our families would not be taken into slavery,
But we would live together neighbourly.

We would no longer have our beautiful gems exploited,
From our land that God has anointed.

Our beautiful continent we love,
Bestowed with precious resources from God above.

Oh if Africa was not colonised!

Daniel Chukwuemeka Duru (13)
Hagley Catholic High School, Hagley

Imagine If They Knew The Real Me

I don't belong at school - no one accepts me
When I try to talk, people laugh and sneer
I get pointed and stared at whenever I walk by
They whisper about me - they think I can't hear

But nobody knows what I had to go through
Maybe they'd act differently
Would they still laugh? Would I have friends?
Imagine if they knew the real me.

I was alone when the bombs first came
My parents were out, I lay awake in bed
Horrible visions filled my mind
I was paralysed with fear and dread.

My mother returned home alone that night
Only by chance had she survived
But the raging fireballs of destruction had hit
My father's office - no one had made it out alive.

The cold hands of my mother shook me awake
Outside, the death-missiles were falling like rain
We packed hurried bags, then ran out the door
Into the world where we couldn't remain

Perched uncomfortably on musty leather seats
A strange man drove us to the outskirts of town
Apprehensions flowed through my veins
And all through this, the bombs rained down.

For hours we lingered in a derelict bus shelter
Surrounded by people, many that we knew
I saw my old nana and friends from my school
They had escaped the danger too.

A miserable journey in a black-windowed bus
Crammed in so tightly that no one could move
But this was the only pathway to freedom
We had hearts full of hope and little to lose

The safe secure boat we'd been promised and paid for,
A patched-up rubber dinghy with room for just three
Yet fifty of us, shoved onto it roughly
Then we travelled away through the stormy black sea.

The voyage was death-defying, perilous and risky
The dark roaring waters, so endless and vast
Huddled between my nana and mother
Knowing every second could be our last.

I fell asleep with my mother's arms around me
But when my eyes opened, I was alone
She was somewhere out there in the deadly black ocean
"Go back!" I screamed sobbing, but we had to go on.

Our hearts lifted when we saw land in the distance
But the surface beneath us began to sink and deflate
Gasping for breath in the icy-cold darkness
Would a watery death be our ultimate fate?

I spotted my nana in the endless grey waters
I clung to her neck as she swam me to shore
For hours we paddled - our arms were both aching
But still we kept swimming, away from the war.

After weeks of travelling and buckets of tears
We arrived in England to be sent to a site
A camp full of people escaping from danger
A safe place to sleep and settle for the night.

A cold draughty tent was our shelter from fear
To fetch drinking water, we'd have to walk miles.
We washed with a bucket - its liquid ice-cold
Clothes lay on the floor in untidy piles.

Then one day a flat became our new home
We lived there for months, just Nana and me
The day that she died, so did my happiness
I was alone in the world - an orphan refugee

A care home took me in like an unwanted parcel
I joined a local school, but didn't fit in
The pain I felt inside captured my body
Why was being different considered such a sin?

Torn from my home like a page from a book
My heart was in Syria, where I should be
But if people knew, would they still act the same?
Imagine if they knew the real me.

Poppy Mullaney (13)
Hagley Catholic High School, Hagley

Imagine If Everyone Who Ever Lived Was Alive Right Now

Imagine if everyone who ever lived was alive right now,
Everyone you knew from different places and times. Would you take a bow?
The world would hold many colours and pleasant aromas, in every corner of the Earth.
Would people feel like it's a new start, a new birth
If everyone who ever lived was alive right now?

Imagine if everyone who ever lived was alive right now
Would there be more destruction, hatred and sadness?
Would this even happen? Would this be allowed?
The world would be a heap of madness
If everyone who ever lived was alive right now

Imagine if everyone who ever lived was alive right now
The many inspirational people would be present,
Leading those around with hope and joy,
If everyone who ever lived was alive right now

Imagine if everyone who ever lived was alive right now
The things that humanity could do together
Stronger than ever before - together as one
If everyone who ever lived was alive right now

Imagine if everyone who ever lived was alive right now
Would everyone feel happy? Would everyone feel love?
Or would there be those who feel blue and grey?
Would they scream and shout to those that would listen?
If everyone who ever lived was alive right now.

Elle Ashe (13)
Hagley Catholic High School, Hagley

Imagine Being Cool Like Her

Imagine being cool like her
Able to hide, able to make mistakes
Behind a laughing plastic face
She can dress like that and
Talk right back
Without fear of consequence

She doesn't seem to have problems
Or fears or insecurities
She doesn't seem real,
I don't understand
That's not normal for me.

How happy she seems!
She can dance and scream,
I could never do that,
Not publicly, no,
I'd do it silently.

She loves herself.
I don't always love me,
I judge myself all the time
She has the confidence
That is impossible to feel.

What makes her so different from me?
The long hair, make-up, mini skirt, and handbag?
Is that it?
She's pretty without that too.
Does she know?

Is that why she can strut?
Because she knows that she looks good,
Underneath all that and on top of it?
She's been out before
I... I don't want romantic love right now.

I don't want a relationship,
I don't want to wear make-up and a mini skirt,
I don't want long hair,
I don't want to be loud,
That's not me.

So if she's happy like that
That's good for her.
I'm me, I prefer my own skin
I come first
This life is not hers, it's mine.

Theresa Collins (13)
Hagley Catholic High School, Hagley

Imagine If Dreams Were Real...

If there was freedom and no rules,
Free things for one and all.
Anything you wish for would come true,
Presents all wrapped up for me and you.
Imagine if dreams were real...

Plates of food lined in front of your eyes,
Chocolate, raspberries and large mince pies.
Sparkling plates of silver and gold,
Lots and lots of food they hold.
Imagine if dreams were real...

Have a power like no one before,
Fire breath, teleporting and much more.
Become a bird and fly high in the sky,
Goodbye to old dreams and to new dreams say hi.
Imagine if dreams were real.

Sofia Iantosca (13)
Hagley Catholic High School, Hagley

Invisible

I magine if you just faded away into thin air.

N obody to talk to. nobody to hear you.

V aporised into the very air we breathe.

I magine if you never even existed to begin with.

S ome figment of someone's imagination.

I nvisible to all.

B elieved in by name.

L ost in somebody's mind.

E ternally lost in time.

Jaymie-Leigh Brennan (16)

John Leggott College, Scunthorpe

Grace

Air pushes past his face
As the heat seems closer.
No sound, only light
He never turns
Never faces back
For he cannot.
Encased by the brightness ahead.

Too close would cause death
But he is too adventurous.
Curiosity killed the cat
But satisfaction brought it back.
Hope is his only salvation

Wings that glow and glisten
A beautiful colour,
The shade of clouds on a summer's day.
They spread far
Large enough to carry a hundred men.
Feathers attached so carefully
To make him graceful.

His ascent was his purpose
His only accomplishment.

As he drew closer he felt too warm
Overwhelmed by the heat.

He did not falter
Graceful always.
Flying continued until he felt it

A slow trickle down his back
Barely there but as hot as could be.
The burn on his back increased
Further and further down.
His back, legs and feet
But he continued.

Only one thing left to do
And do it with grace, he shall.

The wings outstretched for the final
The last chance before descent.
Strength and bravery
Pushed him forward.
However, it isn't enough

The fall doesn't feel rough
It isn't painful,
For his skin is too burnt
To even notice the sharpness of the wind.

A laugh erupts
Not maniacal or dangerous,
One of acceptance.
One of realisation.

Just how foolish was this man
To do an impossible task.

His eyes close
His arms spread wide.
Understanding
No regrets.

You may wonder
Who is this man?

This man's name is...
Icarus,
And he has flown too close to the sun.

Stephanie Papworth (17)
John Leggott College, Scunthorpe

A Study On Human Geology

A pumice stone:
A cold creation of warm ancestors;
A pebble of tension and torment;
A thing from below the surface;

It is brought to smooth, to flatten out:
Those callous extremities from the flesh.
Cause bumps and blemishes to form
Into flat and dusty dunes;

But obscure the flaw as it may,
One single thing comes henceforth:
A crusted coat of rusty red,
A sheet of shattered skin.
Tear and rip and crack and boil
Blood erupts out from within.

So once again the bumps will rise,
Above the shattered crust;
To resume which they whence came:
The cycle of the sin.

Penny Russell (16)
Kingdown Community School, Warminster

Lockdown - A Plague Of Friendship

At first it all seemed so sad,
Shops closed; people got mad,
Schools closed down, we worked from home,
Kids spent their days learning on Chrome.

Wages reduced, money was tight,
Households would argue and they'd fight,
2 metres apart, that was the rule,
No one returned back to school,

But through the dark came a shimmering light,
To guide us through this rainy night,
People began to clap their hands,
The NHS had millions of fans.

Parents and children would go for a walk,
Old friends and colleagues began to talk,
A plague had spread, but in a different way,
A plague of friendship, hip hip hooray!

Not only this, but something amazing would happen,
Far beyond any child could imagine,
The skies grew blue through lockdown weeks,
Now you can see the Himalayan peaks.

Flamingoes painted Mumbai pink,
It gave the world a chance to think,
Goats ran around a seaside town,
Up the beach and then back down.

Whales exploring far and wide,
Families were playing games inside,
Hawaii marine life started to thrive,
People were thankful to be alive.

Communities united in our towns,
Due to the spreading virus crown,
Many were taken, to rest in peace,
Slowly the rate began to decrease.

Let's not forget the friendships we made,
And the countless people who came to our aid,
Key worker, shop keeper and delivery man,
Cleaners keeping hospitals spick and span,

The virus is still out there, please take care,
But the plague of friendship is everywhere.

Tia Daniels (15)
Kingdown Community School, Warminster

Our Climate Has Changed

The burning, blackened earth
like a desert stretching out for miles and miles
or at least, what remains of it
barely existing
through the space-time continuum

no signs of life
as I gaze up to the stars
I remember
how it used to be
so many years ago

animals, wiped out forever.
Humans, three-quarters of the population exterminated.
No sea
no blue sky
all happiness stolen
the air itself burning with the frustration and indignation of
the human race
even though
we brought this on ourselves
We have done this
and now we can't look back.

Vivienne Simcox (12)
Kingdown Community School, Warminster

Imagine A World

Imagine a world
With no family and friends
To love you and keep you

No plants to make the
World look colourful
And beautiful or the crops
And plants we eat
And make into food

No schools to learn
Things we need to
Know in the future
And skills we will
Need to learn if we
Get a job

And finally no Earth
That holds our greatest
Memories and where it
Keeps our loved ones

So we should never
Take stuff for granted
We need to stop destroying
This world.

Danny Loseli (11)
Kingdown Community School, Warminster

Imagine If...

Imagine a world without war
Imagine if we all said no more
Imagine if across the land
We all took a stand
No starving faces
No bombed places
Hatred removed
No war-torn spaces
Imagine together, me and you
United there's nothing we couldn't do
Imagine.

Amber-Rose Cullen (11)
Kingdown Community School, Warminster

Imagine

Imagine a world without stereotypes
Where everyone is treated equally
No more caged birds
And no one lusts for evil.

Maybe it's possible
To live a life without glee
But why can't we do that?
Oh right, because some would 'not agree'.

Perhaps this is false hope
A pitiful cry for help
When the generation fails don't come to me
I was the one to stand and show
But well, none of you believed.

I don't know why I'm doing this
I guess I'm trying to say
Stop the use of stereotypes
And being different...
Well, that's perfectly okay!

Luke Cockle
Landau Forte Academy Amington, Tamworth

Imagine

Imagine for a moment,
A stereotypical world with stereotypical minds,
Imagine,
When the children play together in fantasy worlds,
When moms stay together and dads off hard at work,
Peaceful and the same,
Comfortable and the same,
Oblivious and the same,
Forever and always the same,
Is this how we want it?
Now come back to our non-stereotypical world,
When we eat, do, say, wear, try the latest thing,
That everyone is doing,
Is this how we want it?
Peaceful and the same,
Comfortable and the same,
Oblivious and the same,
Forever and always,
Wrapped up in our own little worlds,
The same,
Is this how we want it?

Lucy Angel Molloy (14)
Landau Forte Academy Amington, Tamworth

Imagine

Imagine a world without stereotypes
Without people judging you
Without people thinking they're different
If the world was ali equal
Everyone would be happy
Everyone would feel human

Why can't we all be equal?
Why can't we accept people?
We are all human
And we all have feelings
Even if people are different
They should be treated equally.

Olivia Statham (13)
Landau Forte Academy Amington, Tamworth

Imagine

Imagine a world with no stereotypes
Where we could be free
How remarkable would that be?

Imagine if no one was judged for what they wore
What they looked like
You could be you
That would be remarkable too.

You could go out without being stared at or laughed at
Can you imagine that?

You wouldn't have to change
Not for anyone.

Libby Ashley
Landau Forte Academy Amington, Tamworth

Imagine A Life With No Disagreement

It would be a dream
With no one being mean
All being friends
Before it all ends
No discrimination
It would all be easier
We'd develop
No one being hidden away
No one in your way
Living an easy life
Not being mice
It would be an easy life!

Seth Cordell
Landau Forte Academy Amington, Tamworth

Someone Told Us

He's a little bit scary
And a bit of a mess
But he's kind and caring
When he's helping the homeless

She's dressed like a princess
All the frills and fur
But her parents have gone without
To get something nice for her.

Ruby Lewis (13)
Landau Forte Academy Amington, Tamworth

Imagine If Kids Ruled The World

If kids ruled the world there wouldn't be any school and no
more homework
We would have more chocolate and more sour sweets
There would be more McDonald's and we could do what we
want
We wouldn't have to pay for anything and we could get
anything for free
We could have lots of chocolate cake and ice cream with
chocolate sauce
We would have ice cream all day and go to the fair and go
on all the rides and not have to pay
We would have lots of doughnuts, candyfloss, s'mores and
hot chocolate with marshmallows in...

Just imagine!

Sophie Howard (11)
Lincoln Castle Academy, Lincoln

Imagine All Your Wishes

Just imagine all your wishes came true just for a day
Imagine you could wish for a dancing hot dog with sprinkles
on top
Or what if you could imagine that the characters from
Among Us were in the real world
That would be amazing if you could wish that.
What if you could make skate budding more fun?
You could even wish for a flying skateboard
Imagine that you could wish for unlimited things for a year
Imagine!

Lilly Killingsworth (12)
Lincoln Castle Academy, Lincoln

Imagine If The Kids Ruled The World

If kids ruled the world
They would tell adults to be slaves
Kids would not have to go to school
Instead, they would do what they liked
If kids ruled the world

Imagine if kids ruled the world
They would not have to go to bed
They would go to bed when they wanted
They could do what they liked
If kids ruled the world

Imagine if kids ruled the world
They would eat what they wanted
To eat chocolate and cake and sweets
McDonald's all day and all things bad
If kids ruled the world.

Kaden Portasman (12)
Lincoln Castle Academy, Lincoln

If Kids Ruled The World, Imagine!

If kids ruled the world
The whole world would be a bin
They would do whatever they want
There would be no rules
If kids ruled the world.

If kids ruled the world there would be no lockdown
No uniform, instead just JD clothes
No arguing about attitude no falling out
There would be no rules
If kids ruled the world

If kids ruled the world
It may not be good
But no hugs from mum, dad or stepdad
No fun and no amazing family time

If kids ruled the world.

Lacey Farnsworth (11)
Lincoln Castle Academy, Lincoln

Scary Dinosaurs

Dinosaurs, dinosaurs, scary dinosaurs
Big dinosaurs fighting in the night
Scary dinosaurs fighting over meat
Triceratops won the fight for the meat
Dinosaurs, dinosaurs.

Dinosaurs, dinosaurs
Imagine there were dinosaurs
Big dinosaurs, scary dinosaurs
A dinosaur at the school
The dinosaurs broke the roof.

Dinosaurs, dinosaurs
They go to the library
To look for food to eat
But be careful, as it is going to eat you!

Carley Barley (11)
Lincoln Castle Academy, Lincoln

Imagine Everything Was Food!

F antastic
O reo
O oze
D elicious

Imagine if everything was edible
if we could eat rain and snow
rain was rainbows
snow was candyfloss.

Imagine if you didn't get sick when you ate lots of sweets
you would never run out but eat them all day and night.
Imagine if turning a tap on made oozing chocolate sauce
it just came out the tap, it would be truly gorgeous.

Just imagine!

Scarlett Richardson (12)
Lincoln Castle Academy, Lincoln

Imagine If You Died Because Of A Coma

Imagine if that tackle in rugby
Really hurt you and you went in a coma
Into a deep sleep
Everyone would be so sad
Imagine if that coma lasted for 5 years
And people thought you were dead
You went in a coffin, but then woke inside
Everyone would be so sad
Imagine if you started screaming and shouting
But no one was there to hear
You gave up and died
Everyone would be so sad.
Imagine.

Bradley Portasman (12)

Lincoln Castle Academy, Lincoln

Imagine Our Dreams Were Real

Imagine our dreams were real
we could imagine there was no one else but us
it would be cool.

Imagine we were not at school
but could go to fun places like the beach,
a restaurant
or a water park.

Imagine our dreams were real!

Sereina Smith (11)
Lincoln Castle Academy, Lincoln

YOUNG WRITERS INFORMATION

We hope you have enjoyed reading this book – and that you will continue to in the coming years.

If you're a young writer who enjoys reading and creative writing, or the parent of an enthusiastic poet or story writer, do visit our website **www.youngwriters.co.uk**. Here you will find free competitions, workshops and games, as well as recommended reads, a poetry glossary and our blog. There's lots to keep budding writers motivated to write!

If you would like to order further copies of this book, or any of our other titles, then please give us a call or order via your online account.

Young Writers
Remus House
Coltsfoot Drive
Peterborough
PE2 9BF
(01733) 890066
info@youngwriters.co.uk

Join in the conversation!
Tips, news, giveaways and much more!

 YoungWritersUK    @YoungWritersCW    @YoungWritersCW